Hello, Family Members,

W9-BVS-137

Learning to read is one of the most important accomplishments of early childhood. **Hello Reader!** books are designed to help children become skilled readers who like to read. Beginning readers learn to read by remembering frequently used words like "the," "is," and "and"; by using phonics skills to decode new words; and by interpreting picture and text clues. These books provide both the stories children enjoy and the structure they need to read fluently and independently. Here are suggestions for helping your child.

- Have your child think about a word he or she does not recognize right away. Provide hints such as "Let's see if we know the sounds" and "Have we read other words like this one?"
- Encourage your child to use phonics skills to sound out new words.
- Provide the word for your child when more assistance is needed so that he or she does not struggle and the experience of reading with you is a positive one.
- Encourage your child to have fun by reading with a lot of expression . . . like an actor!

I do hope that you and your child enjoy this book.

　　　　　—Francie Alexander
　　　　　Reading Specialist,
　　　　　Scholastic's Learning Ventures

Activity Pages

In the back of the book are skill-building activities. These are designed to give children further reading and comprehension practice and to provide added enjoyment. Offer help with directions as needed and encourage your child to have FUN with each activity.

Game Cards

In the middle of the book are eight pairs of game cards. These are designed to help your child become more familiar with words in the book and to play fun games.

- Have your child use the word cards to find matching words in the story. Then have him or her use the picture cards to find matching words in the story.
- Play a matching game. Here's how: Place the cards face up. Have your child match words to pictures. Once the child feels confident matching words to pictures, put cards face down. Have the child lift one card, then lift a second card to see if both match. If the cards match, the child can keep them. If not, place the cards face down once again. Keep going until he or she finds all matches.

For my brother Milo, who loves a good sleep.
—S.B.

For my mother
—G.E.

No part of this publication may be reproduced, or stored in a retrieval system, or transmitted in any form or by any means, electronic, mechanical, photocopying, recording, or otherwise, without written permission of the publisher. For information regarding permission, write to Scholastic Inc., Attention: Permissions Department, 555 Broadway, New York, NY 10012.

ISBN: 0-439-21037-2

Text copyright © 2000 by Samantha Berger.
Illustrations copyright © 2000 by Gloria Elliott.
All rights reserved.   Published by Scholastic Inc.
SCHOLASTIC, HELLO READER, CARTWHEEL BOOKS and associated logos are trademarks and/or registered trademarks of Scholastic Inc.

Library of Congress Cataloging-in-Publication Data available

10 9 8 7 6 5 4 3 2 1   00 01 02 03 04

Printed in the U.S.A.   24
First printing, November 2000

HONK! TOOT! BEEP!

by Samantha Berger
Illustrated by Gloria Elliott

. . . .

My First Hello Reader!
With Game Cards

. . . .

SCHOLASTIC INC.

Cartwheel
B·O·O·K·S®

New York   Toronto   London   Auckland   Sydney
Mexico City   New Delhi   Hong Kong

In the city lived

Milo the Mouse.

He was trying to sleep
in his little mouse house.

But it was too noisy
for a mouse to sleep.

Cars were honking.

Honk! Toot! Beep!

The train was chugging.

Choo, choo, choo!

A police car was chasing.

Woo, woo, woo!

Bikes were racing.

Ring, ring, ring!

A fire truck was rushing.

 **car**

 **train**

 **police car**

 **bike**

fire truck

horse

mouse

house

Ding, ding, ding!

A horse was trotting.

Clop, clop, clop!

Milo yelled,

"THIS NOISE

He moved to the country.
He built a new house.

It was the perfect place

for Milo the Mouse.

On the Go!

Point to all the things that have wheels.
Then say the name of each thing.

Traffic Jam!

This is a big traffic jam!
Point to all the cars.
Point to the bike.
Point to the police car.

Inside Story

Some words have smaller words in them.
In each row, you can use your fingers
to cover a letter or letters in the first word
to make it look like the second word.

trying	**try**
train	**rain**
ring	**in**
honking	**honk**

Letter Match

In each row, point to the word that
begins with the same letter as the
first word in the row.

1. cars   clop   house   noisy

2. train   honk   toot   beep

3. bike   sleep   beep   mouse

4. horse   city   stop   house

5. sleep   train   police   stop

Name That Noise!

Think about the story.

What goes **RING,**
   RING,
     RING?

What goes **CHOO,**
   CHOO,
     CHOO?

What goes **DING,**
   DING,
     DING?

What goes **CLOP,**
   CLOP,
     CLOP?

Let's Get Going!

Here are some different things that go.

Which ones could be real?

Now point to the ones that are make-believe.

ANSWERS

On the Go!

Name That Noise!

The bicycles go RING, RING, RING.

The train goes CHOO, CHOO, CHOC

The fire truck goes DING, DING, DIN(

The horse goes CLOP, CLOP, CLOP.

Let's Get Going!

The car and the bicycle are real.

The banana boat and the can-on-whee
are make-believe.

Letter Match

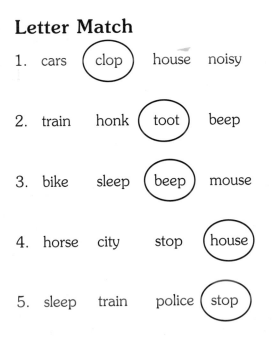

1. cars (clop) house noisy

2. train honk (toot) beep

3. bike sleep (beep) mouse

4. horse city stop (house)

5. sleep train police (stop)